Beast Quest®

ELECTRO
THE STORM BIRD

BY ADAM BLADE

ORCHARD

With special thanks to Tabitha Jones

For Aaron Simpkins

www.beastquest.co.uk

ORCHARD BOOKS

First published in Great Britain in 2019 by The Watts Publishing Group

1 3 5 7 9 10 8 6 4 2

Text © 2019 Beast Quest Limited.
Cover and inside illustrations by Steve Sims
© Beast Quest Limited 2019

Beast Quest is a registered trademark of Beast Quest Limited
Series created by Beast Quest Limited, London

A CIP catalogue record for this book is available from the British Library.

ISBN 978 1 40835 774 3

Printed in Great Britain

The paper and board used in this book are made from wood from responsible sources

Orchard Books
An imprint of Hachette Children's Group
Part of The Watts Publishing Group Limited
Carmelite House, 50 Victoria Embankment, London EC4Y 0DZ

An Hachette UK Company
www.hachette.co.uk
www.hachettechildrens.co.uk

Welcome to the world of Beast Quest!

Tom was once an ordinary village boy, until he travelled to the City, met King Hugo and discovered his destiny. Now he is the Master of the Beasts, sworn to defend Avantia and its people against Evil. Tom draws on the might of the magical Golden Armour, and is protected by powerful tokens granted to him by the Good Beasts of Avantia. Together with his loyal companion Elenna, Tom is always ready to visit new lands and tackle the enemies of the realm.

While there's blood in his veins, Tom will never give up the Quest…

There are special gold coins to
collect in this book. You will earn
one coin for every chapter you read.

Find out what to do with your coins
at the end of the book.

CONTENTS

Banners fly from the walls of King Hugo's Palace and all Avantia rejoices at Tom's latest victory. The people worship the snivelling wretch as if he's their saviour.

Well, forgive me if I'm not bowing down. He killed my father Sanpao and drove my mother Kensa from the kingdom.

So, in revenge, I'm going to spoil their little party.

Soon Avantia will face a Beast like no other.

And when they look for their little hero to save their skins, he will be nowhere to be found.

Ria

1

A DAY LONG
AWAITED

Tom sat straight-backed on the
raised dais near the king and queen,
his stomach churning with nerves
as he gazed over the crowded
courtyard. The jewelled outfits
and dress armour of the assembled
guests shone in the morning sun,
dazzling him. A fresh breeze made

the palace flags ripple and snap overhead, and colourful bunting fluttered all along the courtyard walls.

"I'm not used to all this attention," Tom muttered to Elenna, who sat close by his side. Most of the court and palace guard had assembled to watch him receive his powers back. Even his aunt and uncle had come all the way from Errinel. When he caught Aunt Maria's eye, she waved, her face glowing with pride.

"You've earned it," Elenna whispered. "If we hadn't got the Circle of Wizards' artefacts back from the Locksmith, goodness knows what trouble we'd be facing

now. Restoring your powers is the
least they could do."

Tom had to agree she was right. The
Circle's stolen items had accidentally
released a fiery Beast called
Scalamanx that he'd had to defeat.

"Will the magic lot ever turn up?"
grumbled Captain Harkman, from
his station just behind them. "It is
unforgivable to keep the king and
queen waiting like this."

A sudden flash of white light
blinded Tom, and startled yelps and
gasps ran through the crowd. When
Tom's vision cleared, he saw two
figures in flowing purple gowns
edged with gold, standing on the dais
before Hugo and Aroha – Sorella,

the head of the Circle, and a young
wizard, Stefan. Beside them, two
burly men in armour carried a hefty-
looking chest. The king and queen
smiled welcomingly, but Sorella
and Stefan turned away to face the

crowd without giving them so much as a nod.

"Insolence!" Harkman growled.

Sorella lifted a hand, waiting for silence. Then she spoke in a solemn voice: "After a long and valiant struggle, setting aside all personal comforts for the good of Avantia, this day has finally come," she said. "Few have sacrificed so much. Few have striven with such courage in the face of adversity." Sorella paused to gather her audience, and Elenna nudged Tom.

"See?" she murmured. "Even Sorella knows you're a hero."

"But we have finally succeeded where others would have failed!" Sorella cried.

Elenna made a choking sound and Tom felt himself flush. *I should have known she'd be talking about herself...*

The witch clicked her fingers,

and immediately, Tom's shield
and belt appeared across Stefan's
outstretched arms. *Oohs* and *ahhhs*
rippled through the crowd. Stefan

turned to Tom, smiling smugly, but Tom sprang up to meet the wizard, joy surging through him as he ran his fingers over the familiar shape of each magical token and jewel. He slung the shield over his shoulder and strapped on his belt, then stood tall.

Now I can serve Avantia properly again!

Sorella gestured to the two guards holding the chest. "The Circle of Wizards have fulfilled their promise," she said. "It took many days to re-forge the Golden Armour. We have even improved on the original design." The two men stepped aside, and Stefan slowly opened the chest, a haughty smirk on his face. Tom felt his heart skip as the sunlight reflected off his gleaming armour.

Relief flooded through him as he bent and lifted the breastplate, feeling the cool weight of it in his hands. Elenna was at his side in an instant, helping him with the buckles. Tom noticed that the armour felt lighter, and as Elenna helped him fit the arm and leg pieces, he found he could flex his knees and elbows as easily as if he wasn't wearing armour at all. Finally, he set the helmet on his head. A sudden, welcome rush of heat filled his limbs and chest. *My magical powers are back!* Tom drew his sword and brandished it, amazed by the strength the new armour gave him – his sword felt weightless.

A huge cheer erupted from the crowd. Tom grinned and made a thrust with his blade, then gave a couple of quick turns and jabs, each to riotous applause. But as Tom dropped into a lunge, his armour seemed to tighten, squeezing his chest so hard he could barely breathe. His blood pulsed loud in his ears and his vision blurred.

"Tom! What's wrong?" Elenna cried. Tom tried to speak, but only managed a choking wheeze. Muffled cries of alarm and screams from the crowd pierced his muddled senses. Tom looked down to see an inky

black stain spreading across the
metal of his breastplate, starting
from the centre of his chest. As
the black reached his arm and leg

armour, blazing agony shot through his limbs. Pain knifed through his head and all the colour drained from his vision, leaving only shades of black and grey. His body spasmed and he fell clattering to the ground, clawing at his throat as he gasped for breath.

Elenna's face swam into focus. "Tom?" she cried, scrabbling at his helmet, tugging it free – but still, he felt as if strong hands were strangling him. His breastplate crushed the last of the air from his body. As his senses began to fade, he suddenly spotted a hooded girl near the front of the crowd. The sun glinted off the silver hoop through the girl's ear, and her green eyes blazed with hatred. Even with his failing vision, Tom would recognise her anywhere. *Ria*. The daughter of two of Tom's mortal enemies – the dead Pirate King Sanpao, and the Evil Witch Kensa. *What has she done to me?*

With his last strength, he lifted his hand and pointed towards her.

He heard Elenna shouting as darkness closed over him and he sank into oblivion.

CORRUPTED MAGIC

"Tom! What's happening to you?"
Elenna shouted frantically, heart
clenched in horror. Kneeling at his
side, she watched as his eyes rolled
back into his head. His body began
to shake in a violent fit. She tried
to hold him down as white froth
dribbled from his mouth. Sweeping
her eyes over the length of his body,

she saw that the armour had turned fully black and had the dull lustre of coal. *Did the Circle's magic go wrong?* she thought. *Is it killing him?*

Tom's body fell suddenly still. With sickening dread, Elenna placed an ear to his mouth. She heard shallow rasps of breath flickering across his lips. *He's alive, just.* She noticed his arm lay outstretched where he had tried to raise it a moment before. *Was he trying to show me something?* She followed its direction, catching sight of a slender, hooded figure standing in the crowd. With a hot rush of fury, Elenna recognised who it was. "Ria!" she shouted.

The pirate girl shot Elenna a

spiteful grin, then turned to shove
her way through the guests, towards
the courtyard gate. Elenna started to
stand up, but then fell back, torn.
I can't leave Tom!

"Wake up!" Elenna cried, shaking
Tom, but he didn't respond. Daltec
dropped to Tom's side and gripped
his wrist, feeling for a pulse.

"I'll see to him!" Daltec said. "You
follow Ria!" Swallowing her rising
panic, Elenna shot to her feet.

"Captain Harkman!" Elenna cried,
pointing after Ria. "We have to stop
her!" Elenna leaped from the dais
and bundled after the retreating
witch. Wide-eyed men and women
dived out of her path as she ran. She

tried to string an arrow and take aim, but it was too risky to shoot with so many people in the way.

"Men!" Harkman boomed. "After the girl in the hood!" Elenna heard the clamour of running armoured men from all around her. Ahead, Ria had almost reached the main gate. Two guards crossed swords, blocking the exit, but Ria drew her crackling cat-o'-nine-tails and sent its fizzing tips lashing towards one then the other. The blows sent the guards flying out of Ria's path, their armour sizzling with light. They crashed to the ground, clutching their chests.

Elenna raced on, but she knew she'd never make it in time. Ria sped

through the archway, cracking her
whip at the chain of the portcullis,
severing it. Elenna reached the arch
just as Ria dived under the falling
iron gates. The gate hit the ground

with a clang, right in front of Elenna.
Casting one last venomous smirk
back over her shoulder, Ria sped off.

Elenna stood close by Tom's bedside.
*Please, Tom, show me some sign
you're still in there...* He lay perfectly
still, his skin the translucent white
of bone china. The branching veins
along his throat stood out, and were
black instead of blue. Elenna blinked
back tears. Clad in the strange dark
armour, he looked like the carved
statue on the tomb of a knight. Aduro
stood near Elenna with Daltec and
King Hugo, holding Tom's blackened
helmet in his arms. On the far side of

the bed, Tom's aunt Maria held one of his hands, brushing his palm with her thumb, while his uncle Henry stood at her side. Sorella and Stefan watched sombrely from the foot of the bed.

Daltec muttered another unlocking spell under his breath, then tried for the fifth time to loosen the buckles securing Tom's breastplate. Immediately, Tom started to writhe, a thin moan of pain escaping his clenched teeth.

Daltec made a swift cutting motion with his hand, ending the spell. Tom fell still. "It's too dangerous to continue," Daltec said, his brows pinched together with worry. "The armour is magically fused to his body.

If I keep going, the strain could kill him."

Elenna's heart gave a painful squeeze. Maria started to weep.

"Ria must somehow have

corrupted the forging process for the armour!" Hugo growled.

"Impossible!" Stefan sneered. "I oversaw the entire process myself."

"Just like you oversaw the security of your secret vault when the Locksmith stole everything?" Hugo snapped.

"Well, I—" Stefan started indignantly, but Sorella cut in.

"Hugo is a king, Stefan, and deserves your respect. And no matter how closely you watched the forging process, it is clear something has gone amiss, wouldn't you say?"

Stefan scowled, but didn't answer.

As she looked down at Tom, watching his chest barely rise and fall, Elenna's anger flared. "It doesn't matter whose fault it is," she said. "We have to do something to help him!"

"I think I may be able to create an antidote," Aduro said, "but it will take time, and I don't know how long Tom may have."

"You are no longer permitted to practise magic!" Stefan said, one eyebrow arched as he gazed down his nose at the old wizard.

Aduro's grey eyes sparked with fury. "You may be able to stand idly by and watch a young hero perish," he said, "but I can't! Now, if you have nothing more useful to offer, I'll get started." He held Stefan's eyes for a long moment, until the younger wizard lowered his gaze. Aduro swept from the room.

Maria bent and brushed Tom's hair back from his pale face. "Stay with us," she said. Then she looked up at the king. "I've sent word to his mother in Gwildor. I asked her to come quickly. If Tom doesn't pull through..." Maria's voice faltered. Henry put his arm around his wife's shoulders.

"Tom's the strongest, bravest boy I know," he said. "He'll pull through."

Elenna looked at Tom's pale skin lined with raised black veins, wanting badly to believe Henry's words. But all she could feel was a cold and empty dread. *He doesn't know what Ria's capable of...*

Suddenly Tom's body jerked into motion, shuddering all over. Elenna touched his arm, trying to still him, but the shudders built quickly to a wild thrashing. Henry gripped Tom's shoulders, but Tom sat bolt upright, wrenching free of his uncle's grip.

His eyes flicked open.

A slow smile spread across his face.

"Tom, are you all right?" Elenna cried, feeling a surge of hope. But Tom stared blankly ahead, still wearing the fixed, eerie grin. He closed his eyes briefly. When he opened them again, Elenna gasped, reeling back.

Tom's eyes had turned black. All black. They narrowed to inky slits as he turned to face her.

"Tom?" Elenna breathed, unable to keep the quiver out of her voice.

Tom said nothing. He leaped from the bed, shoving her so hard she slammed into the wall behind her and fell sprawling to the ground.

"Tom, stop!" Maria cried, but Tom ignored her. Elenna scrambled up to see Daltec and Hugo rush to intercept him, but Tom dipped his shoulder and knocked them aside before dashing out of the room.

Elenna raced past the others. She skidded into the corridor to see Tom running with magical speed straight at a stained-glass window, as if he was going to run through it.

The fall will kill him! Elenna thought, as Tom bent his knees and sprang, smashing through the window, sending a burst of glittering shards outwards and vanishing.

Elenna reached the window, shaking all over, and made herself look down. But instead of the broken body she had expected to find, she saw her best friend drifting slowly over the palace gardens, holding his shield above him. *Arcta's feather*, Elenna realised. Then she spotted something else – a large dark shape speeding towards Tom with powerful wing thrusts. *A flying horse!*

With a proud neigh, the winged stallion dived through the air,

swooping beneath Tom, who dropped
lightly on to the creature's back in
mid-flight and grabbed the reins.
Then, without looking back, he gave
the reins a vicious snap, kicked the
horse's sides and sped away.

1

3

A HEART TURNED DARK

Tom's blood beat loud in his ears as the winged horse carried him swiftly over fields and villages far below. The bright golds and greens of the countryside made his head hurt, and he urged the horse onwards with a sharp jab of his heels, eager to reach the stark and empty mountains of the north.

He spotted a group of villagers as tiny as insects gathering wheat into hayricks while their children played nearby. The sight of them, happy and oblivious, filled Tom with rage. *They tend their fields, safe and ignorant, while I face death again and again... and for what? An early grave like my father, most likely. Well, not any more.*

Eventually, the sickeningly pretty cottages and fields gave way to more rugged terrain. Tom drew a breath of relief. A thick blanket of grey cloud hid the sun, easing his aching head, and a strong, cold wind gusted between the high peaks. The violence of the wind revived him. He balled his fists on his horse's reins and gritted his teeth. *The people of Avantia will pay for how they have treated me*, he vowed.

As they neared a mountain range, the flying steed banked, swooping towards a dark cave high on a steep, jagged slope. The horse's hooves clattered down just inside the cave. Tom slid from the saddle. Glistening wet shards of grey rock seamed with quartz jutted up from the cavern floor, and water trickled down the walls. In the centre of the cave, on an elevated throne carved from the glittering stone, sat Tom's new mistress, her chin held high and her eyes bright.

"Kneel," Ria said.

Tom started to bend his knee, but froze halfway to the ground, a wave of vertigo washing over him. Hazy memories swam in his mind. A girl with a mohawk trying to kill him. A pirate king disappearing beneath pounding waves...

He quickly shook the thoughts away. *Ria is powerful and ruthless – only she can lead me in my Quest for revenge.*

Tom knelt and bowed his head. "My mistress," he said.

He looked up to see her smiling. "I know how much you have always enjoyed a Quest," Ria said. "Well, I

have one for you. Have you ever heard
of a Beast called Krokol?"

Tom frowned, trying to cast his mind
back to his studies, but he found his
memory strangely blank. And yet the

name seemed somehow familiar.

"Vaguely," he said.

"Well, you'll know him far better than that soon," Ria said. "Krokol was a Beast born from one man's lust for power in the land of Pyloris. He almost destroyed the whole kingdom, before Avantia dispatched its first Master of the Beasts, Tanner, to deal with him."

Tanner... Tom knew that name, for sure. *Another of my ancestors who died on a fool's Quest!* "Did he succeed?" he asked.

"Not quite..." Ria said. She waved a hand at the crystal-seamed wall behind her, and a vision took shape, translucent so that Tom could still

see the water-slick rock behind it. It
showed a warrior clad in the Golden
Armour, gripped in the fist of a giant
Beast shaped like a man, but hairy
and bow-legged with fangs instead
of teeth.

"Tanner and Krokol fought to a stalemate," Ria said. "But Tanner had dipped his sword in a potion made by his wizard, Rufus. He managed to infect Krokol, but was badly wounded in the attempt. Rufus's potion split Krokol into three smaller Beasts. But rather than fight them as a hero should, Tanner fled back to Avantia to tend his injuries." Ria waved her hand once more, and the tableau of man and Beast vanished. She fixed her eyes on Tom.

"I want you to kill all three of Krokol's Beasts and bring the tokens they leave behind to me," she said.

"Why?" Tom asked.

Ria waved a hand dismissively.

"That doesn't concern you," she said. Then she shrugged. "You'll probably die in the attempt anyway, but I suppose it's worth a try."

Tom tensed, anger flashing through him. *Why should I put my life at risk?* he thought. But as Ria watched him, her green eyes narrowing impatiently, he felt his rage flare against Avantia instead. *At least Ria's honest with me*, Tom thought. *She doesn't pretend to care about me as she uses me as her pawn. And I know she'll use the tokens to weaken my real enemy – the people who sent my father to die, and who send me again and again into danger, not caring whether I ever return home...*

"I'll do it," he said.

Ria smiled, then stepped down from her throne of rock. She crossed to a narrow fissure in the cavern wall and reached inside, drawing out a long, silver staff engraved with swirling patterns. *The lightning staff*, Tom realised, his pulse quickening. *She's going to open a portal.*

Ria lifted the staff high and started to chant, her eyes fixed on the mouth of the cave. Instantly, the light dimmed, and a powerful wind gusted around them. From near the opening, Ria's horse let out a snort of unease. Tom turned to see vast, dark clouds boiling in the sky, fattening and darkening, quickly becoming huge, black thunderheads. He opened his arms, feeling the energy of the storm buffeting against him.

Ria's eyes rolled up as she chanted a few last shrill words. Forked lightning lashed towards her, striking the tip of the staff, bleaching the rocks all around her so they stood like pale, jagged teeth. Ria aimed the crackling tip of the lightning staff towards the glistening wall, letting out a guttural cry.

Boom! A swirling portal opened in the rock, purple and black – a spinning vortex of shadow.

"Come," Ria said, moving towards the portal. She clicked her fingers, and the winged stallion stepped to

her side. Tom felt the darkness of
the portal drawing him irresistibly
towards it, like the pull of a riptide
at sea. He started forward…

"Tom, stop!" a voice shouted. He
glanced towards the cave entrance to

see a short-haired girl and a cloaked youth standing there. A strange rush of emotions welled up inside him, a mixture of sickness and confusion. But they quickly gave way to anger as he remembered their names.

Elenna and Daltec. They will try to
return me to my old life as Avantia's
slave!

"He's loyal to me now," Ria called
to Elenna, stepping back towards the
portal.

"Never!" Elenna cried, lifting her

bow and aiming an arrow at Ria.

A rage like nothing he'd felt before burned inside Tom's chest. He threw himself before his mistress, using his armoured body to shield her.

"Move aside, Tom!" Elenna said, her jaw set and her eyes narrowed as she focussed along her arrow.

Tom shook his head. "Not while there's blood in my veins."

Then Ria grabbed his arm, and tugged him backwards into swirling darkness.

THE GATE TO PYLORIS

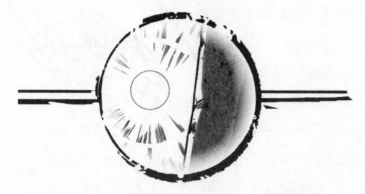

Crowded around a table in Aduro's chamber, along with Daltec and Sorella, Elenna recounted all that had happened. "The portal closed before we got through," she finished, blinking away the tears that prickled in her eyes.

Aduro rubbed a hand over his

lined face. His skin looked grey with exhaustion and his eyes were sorrowful and grave. Even Sorella had lost her sneer.

"How will we find him?" Daltec asked. "The portal was black, so we have no idea where he went."

"I've tested Tom's blood," Aduro said. "It is infected with the blood of Krokol – an ancient Beast from the land of Pyloris. Tanner once fought Krokol and managed to turn him into three less powerful Beasts. They still roam Pyloris now, so that would be the obvious place to look first. Unfortunately, the incantation Tanner's wizard used to open a portal to that realm has long been lost to time..."

A sudden idea struck Elenna and she felt a flicker of hope. "What about the Locksmith's keys?" she asked Sorella. "When you catalogued them, did you find a key for Pyloris?"

Sorella frowned and shook her head. "Even if there were such a key, the Circle would never permit—"

Elenna brought her fist down hard on the table. "It's the Circle's fault Tom's been enchanted!" she cried. "The least you can do is help us find him."

Sorella let out a sigh and turned to Stefan, who stood by Aduro's fire.

"Fetch the keys," she told him. The young wizard looked for a moment as if he might argue, but Sorella struck her staff on the ground. Stefan spun on his heel and stalked from the room, muttering angrily under his breath. Elenna heard something about "broken rules".

Rules! she thought. *How can he care about rules at a time like this?*

Elenna stood ready in the courtyard beside the stable doors, gripping Storm's reins tightly. The black stallion whickered and flicked his ears.

Elenna stroked his flank. "We'll find Tom," she whispered, trying to calm herself as much as the horse.

Aduro had explained that Pyloris was a desert land prone to sandstorms, so Elenna had packed the stallion's saddlebags with dried food and plenty of water and wore a long shawl around her neck. Now all she needed was the key to open the portal, and Aduro's antidote. *Please hurry!*

At last, Sorella rounded the corner of a barn and hurried towards Elenna with Stefan at her side.

"I have them," Sorella said, holding out a pair of large keys.

Elenna took them, feeling the cool weight of the metal in her palm. "Thank you," she said. "I hope this works!"

"Of course they will work," Stefan

snapped. "And don't forget, they remain the property of the Circle of Wizards. You're just borrowing the keys."

Elenna took a deep breath, forcing herself to stay calm. A moment later, she spotted Daltec hurrying towards them, bundled in a travelling cloak and carrying a knapsack.

The young wizard stopped before her, panting. "Ah! I'm not too late," he said.

"Surely you're not coming too?" Elenna asked, hardly daring to hope. "Won't you be needed here, defending the kingdom?"

"There is nothing better I can do for the kingdom than help you find Tom and cure his enchantment," Daltec said. "Avantia needs its Master of the Beasts. And I need to know I've done everything I can to help my friend." Daltec rummaged in his bag and drew out a small flat disc. When he held it out between them, Elenna saw it was Tom's magic compass, but the golden needle had been replaced with a dull, black one which swung wildly about.

"I've rigged Tom's compass with a piece of his enchanted helmet," Daltec said. "When we get to Pyloris, the needle should be attracted to the rest of Tom's armour. Evil attracts Evil," he added, sadly. "It will lead us to him."

Finally, Aduro arrived, hobbling across the flagstones, leaning heavily on his staff. "The antidote is ready, but you must leave at once,"

he said, taking a slender vial from his cloak. It was filled with a viscous black liquid. "Somehow, you will need to get Tom to swallow some of this – but I fear he will be less than willing."

Elenna took the vial and slipped it into her tunic pocket. "Thank you," she said. "I'll make sure he drinks it." But, remembering how easily Tom had shrugged off Henry's grip and escaped from his sickbed, she couldn't think how.

Steeling herself, Elenna slotted the key into the stable lock. *Please work!* To her relief, the key turned smoothly, opening the door with a soft click. As she pushed the door

wider, a scorching wind gusted
into her face, like the blast from a
hot oven. Through the open door,
she could see rippled dunes of pale

yellow sand, half-hidden by swirling
eddies of dust.

I'm coming, Tom! Elenna thought
to herself.

5

A CIVILISATION IN RUINS

Leaning over the back of the winged stallion behind his mistress, Tom gazed down at the Kingdom of Pyloris. A dry wind buffeted against him, offering little relief from the scorching heat. Already his throat felt parched. Spread below, the wind-blasted remains of ancient

buildings poked up from the sand like half-buried skeletons.

Dust devils whirled over the parched terrain and a heat haze made the huge, crumbling pyramids in the distance shimmer.

"What happened to this place?" Tom asked.

"Krokol happened," Ria said. "Long ago, Pyloris was renowned for its culture and its scientific discoveries. But the last king of Pyloris was a fool. He dabbled with magic he didn't understand and created a Beast to destroy his enemies. Of course, the Beast had other ideas. Krokol turned on the people, starting with the king, and didn't stop until everyone was dead."

Squinting down through swirling clouds of sand, Tom thought he could see what looked like the glint of sun on steel…and movement among the shadowy ruins. "Maybe not everyone…" he muttered, then gasped as dozens of figures with long blood-red hair sprang from hiding places. "Watch out!" Tom cried.

Ria cursed and tugged the reins as the people below brandished weapons. Some waved spears and rusty-looking swords, while others held what looked like pipes to their lips. Tom heard the whizz of missiles streaming past him. *Blowpipes!* he realised, too late. Ria yelped, then slumped forward over the winged horse's mane, a small dart sticking from her neck.

Tom plucked the barb from Ria's skin and grabbed the reins, steering upwards. But as he drove his heels into the stallion's sides, it squealed. The horse's wingbeats faltered and it lurched sideways. *It's been hit too!* Clinging tightly with his knees, Tom positioned his shield to protect himself from the poisoned darts, then braced his muscles for a fall. The stallion's eyes rolled up in its head and its wings beat unevenly, then, with a final pathetic flutter, Tom felt its body go slack. His stomach lurched as the horse plummeted towards the sand.

Below, the desert folk crowded together, letting out shrill, eager cries. As the dunes drew close, Tom tried to throw himself from the

saddle, but his boot caught in the stirrup and he crashed down into the sand, grunting with pain as the weight of the stallion came down on his legs. Ria landed nearby, thrown from the saddle, her eyes still closed.

"Cage them!" a harsh voice cried. Tom squirmed and struggled, trying to free himself from the crushing weight of the stallion slumped across his legs. But it was no good. A crowd of hollow-cheeked people swarmed towards him and Ria. All of them, men and women alike, had long scarlet hair and emerald-green eyes, and their clothes hung loose as if they hadn't eaten properly in many days. All except one – a muscular, bare-chested man holding a long staff. His head was as bald as an egg. Gold and jewels shone around his neck and wrists.

"Leave her alone!" Tom cried, as a group of half-starved looking men and women fell on Ria, grabbing her by the arms and legs and lifting her up. He twisted, reaching for his sword, but it was pinned to his thigh under the horse.

Ragged people gripped his armpits and hauled him out. More took his legs. He craned his neck to see Ria bobbing alongside him, being carried towards what looked like a pair of horned rhinos with iron cages on their backs.

Tom felt dazed from the crash-landing. He thrashed and kicked with all the strength of his breastplate, knocking two of his captors away, but others quickly took their places.

"Stop that!" the bare-chested shaman snapped, and swung his staff, cracking Tom across the temple. With a flash of pain, Tom's vision blanked, and he felt himself hefted inside one of the cages. The door slammed shut with a clang.

Tom sat up and shook his head to clear the dizziness. The sight of the desert folk gaping up at him filled him with rage. He sprang forward and gripped the bars. "I'll kill you all when I get out of here!" Tom growled. His captors reeled back, their faces etched with terror, but the bald shaman scowled, pointing his staff at them.

"He can't hurt you, you cowards,"

he shouted. "Now get moving!"

The rhino bearing Tom's cage
lurched into a heavy-footed trot,
jolting him so he almost fell. As he
was bumped and jerked over the
baking dunes, he glanced back to

see Ria's rhino plodding behind his own, while the red-haired desert people followed. He gritted his teeth, his chest burning with fury. *How dare they lay hands on my mistress?* he thought. *I'll break their bones!*

At last, the jolting ride came to a halt at the base of a high sandstone pyramid. Looking up the stepped sides, Tom could see the silhouette of a great carved bird right at the top, its wings outstretched, and its long, sharp beak raised towards the sky.

In her cage, Ria sat up, rubbing her eyes. She glanced about at the desert people gathered around her.

"I could do with some water!" she croaked.

The bare-headed shaman shrugged.
"There is no water," he said. "Our
wells have all run dry." Then he
smirked. "But Electro will bring us
storms and great rains...just as soon
as she has her sacrifice."

Tom's own throat felt so dry, it hurt to swallow. He thought of their meagre water supplies, left behind with their unconscious horse. "Then hadn't you better get on with it?" he said.

The man tipped back his head and laughed. Somewhere, a drum began to beat. Ria shot Tom a scornful look. "*We're* the sacrifice, you fool!" she snapped.

Tom suddenly felt cold, despite the heat. He swallowed. *A sacrifice to what?*

6

ELECTRO'S TRIBUTE

Elenna pulled her scarf away from her mouth and took another swig from her bottle. The tepid water moistened her chapped lips but did little to quench her thirst. She already felt sick and dizzy from the heat. But with no way of knowing how long they had left to travel, she didn't dare drink more. She poured some water into a leather bowl and held it out to Storm, then handed the flask to Daltec.

Daltec took a sip and tucked the bottle back into the saddlebag. Then he drew Tom's compass from his pocket and held it out on the flat of his hand. Elenna watched the black needle swing back and forth, then settle, pointing towards a pyramid in the distance.

"Looks like we have to keep going that way," Daltec said.

Elenna nodded and gave Storm's reins a gentle tug. They trudged onwards, passing the wind-blasted ruins of sandstone buildings.

Looking at the stumps of broken
columns and worn carvings that
remained, Elenna realised they must

have once been grand. But now they lay half-buried, their insides open to the wind.

"What are these buildings?" Elenna asked.

"They are all that is left of Pyloris," Daltec said.

After that, they walked in silence. Elenna's head soon throbbed and shimmering mirages hovered before her. It took all her concentration just to keep moving over the endless dunes.

Then suddenly, through the shifting heat haze, Elenna noticed something different up ahead – a group of small domed huts.

"We should be wary," Daltec said

shading his eyes and gazing towards them. "That looks like a modern settlement."

Elenna drew her bow from her back. As they neared the huts, she saw they were little more than animal skins held up with bones. And nothing moved among the makeshift buildings – not so much as a starved rat. A bleached ram's skull lay on the ground, along with a grinding stone and the blackened remains of a cookfire outside one of the huts. But nothing else. The site was deserted.

"The people must have been here recently," Elenna said, gesturing towards the circle of ashes.

"And look!" Daltec said, pointing. A small well stood at the far side of the site. Storm's ears pricked up eagerly as they approached it. But when Elenna looked inside, she saw nothing except a few stones.

"Whoever lived here must have left in search of water," Elenna said, as a strong gust of wind whipped at her scarf, and the sunlight dimmed.

Daltec gasped and gripped her arm, his eyes on the horizon. Elenna followed his gaze to see clouds forming right above the distant pyramid, spreading outwards with unnatural speed, boiling upwards into dark, towering columns. Another gust of wind hit them,

heavy with the scent of rain. Storm
snorted and flicked his tail.

"This feels like dark magic to me,"
Daltec muttered.

Elenna turned her back to the wind so she'd be heard. "Whatever's going on seems to centre on that pyramid," she said. A clap of thunder rumbled in the distance, long and low, like the roar of a Beast. "And that's where the compass says Tom is. Let's hurry!"

Elenna climbed on to Storm's back and Daltec swung up behind her. With a tap of her heels the stallion leaped off at a gallop, straight into the ferocious wind. The buffeting gusts made it hard for Elenna to breathe, and sand found its way into her eyes and throat despite her scarf. Storm's flanks heaved as he raced over the desert.

Elenna wished they could stop to let him rest, but she knew they couldn't. Tom's life was at stake.

When they finally neared the pyramid, Elenna's sense of foreboding deepened. Shadowy figures hurried about near the base of the structure, while lightning lashed around its tip. Flash after flash illuminated a statue of a great bird perched at the pyramid's peak, its broad wings spread wide. Between the thunderclaps, Elenna could hear the steady beat of drums.

A great bolt of lightning struck the statue, and chunks of stone flaked away, revealing gleaming wings and a shining skeleton, all made of metal.

The wings flexed, beating hard, and more stone fell away. Elenna gasped. *The statue's alive!*

"Electro!" Daltec cried. Elenna stared, taking in the bird's long, razor-sharp beak and lightning blue eyes. With a flap of her purple-silver wings the Beast took off, circling the top of the pyramid to gasps and cries from the crowd below. The last flakes of stone tumbled from her body. A fork of lightning zigzagged towards her, hitting her body with a crack. Her eyes blazed brighter than ever as if energised by the strike.

"Electro is one of the three Children of Krokol," Daltec said.

As Elenna tore her eyes from the

huge bird and looked at the people surrounding the pyramid, she saw something that filled her with horror.

"There's Tom!" she cried, pointing.

At the base of the pyramid, thin hunched figures with blood-red hair surrounded a wooden scaffold structure that looked a lot like a gallows. Dangling from the scaffold by his feet, still wearing his pitch-black armour, hung Tom, beside Ria.

Fat, heavy raindrops started to fall, spattering the sand with dark splotches and filling the air with a musty scent. The people by the pyramid howled in delight and threw back their heads, arms raised and mouths open to catch the downpour.

The rain fell thicker and faster. The thud of the drums became wild. Near where Tom hung, a bare-chested man raised a wooden staff. He threw back his head and opened his arms, letting the rain stream down his skin.

"We give thanks!" the man cried loudly, his voice rising above the beat of the drums and the driving rain. "Electro has sent us the rain we prayed for. Now! Claim your tribute!"

A chant started up from the gathered people. "Electro! Electro! Electro!" Elenna glanced up to see the great bird diving straight towards Tom and Ria, her beak gaping wide.

Elenna lifted her bow, taking aim at the slender ropes that held Tom and Ria above the ground. The rain pelted down, blurring her vision as fast as she could blink it away. Her heart beat wildly in her chest, but somehow she held her bow steady.

If I miss, then Tom will die, Elenna told herself. *So I can't miss!*

THE HEART OF THE STORM

"I expected more from you!" Ria growled, her shoulder pressed against Tom's as they hung upside down. Even amid the chaos of chanting and drums, her words stung Tom like a whip. He fixed his eyes on the giant metal bird swooping towards them. Its mouth gaped hungrily and its eyes crackled with blue fire. Tom clenched his teeth. *I've failed my mistress. I may as well die!*

Suddenly, Tom heard a *swoosh* and a *twang*. His stomach flipped as he plummeted towards the desert. He landed in wet sand, still tangled with Ria, grunting with pain as her elbow jabbed into his gut. Tom rolled away and staggered up, the frayed rope still trailing from his ankle. Ria stood and lurched away from him just as the great silver Beast let out a shriek of fury and sped by overhead.

"Capture them!" the shaman cried from his platform. Soaked to the skin, the desert folk looked more pathetic than ever. Tom hunkered down, ready to fight, but all his opponents had their eyes fixed on their leader, their mouths hanging open with alarm. Tom glanced up to see Electro swooping for the shaman's platform, her silver beak wide open.

The shaman threw up his hands. "Please, no...I beg you!" he cried in a trembling voice as the Beast sped towards him.

SNAP! The giant bird swallowed him whole.

Cries of terror went up from the gathered people. At once, they began running in every direction.

"Tom!" Ria cried. He glanced over to see her standing at the bottom of the wooden scaffold. His shield lay at her feet. She held her cat-o'-nine-tails in one hand and his sword in her other.

Ria sent the sword spinning towards Tom. He snatched it from the air. She tossed him his shield. Brandishing his weapons, he glanced around at the retreating desert people. A pasty youth with a pockmarked face lurched towards him, his eyes wild and his hands raised. Tom lunged with his sword, ready to cut the fool in half.

Before Tom could land the blow, someone slammed into his back

and bundled him down on to the wet sand. Growling with fury, Tom struggled free of his attacker's grip. *Elenna!* The girl scrambled up to face him, her chest heaving and her hair plastered to her head with rain.

"What are you doing?" she cried as the youth scrambled away. "These people are unarmed and practically starving!"

"Then I'll put them out of their misery," Tom said, feeling a surge of satisfaction when he saw the look of horror on her face.

"You're not Evil, Tom!" Elenna cried, aiming an arrow at his chest. "I won't let you hurt them!" Another crack of thunder boomed overhead. More thuds and bangs quickly followed, along with screams of terror from the desert people who milled around like panicked chickens.

"Elenna!" Tom heard Daltec shout.

"We've got bigger problems right now!"Tom glanced Daltec's way to see the young wizard pointing up at Electro. The bird's metal body crackled with lightning and her eyes shone so brightly that it hurt Tom to look at them. And as he watched, forks of lightning shot from the tips of Electro's talons and lashed towards him. Tom lifted his shield.

BOOM! A bolt of lightning slammed into the wood, flinging him backwards. He landed on his back, his hands fizzing with pain. Wet sand pelted down on top of him and his ears were filled with terrified screams and wails.

"Tom! Can't you hurry up and defeat that thing?" Ria shrieked.

Tom sat up and shook his head to clear his vision. "How?" he asked, shouting to be heard over the chaos all around them.

Ria scowled back at him, sand spattered all over her face and clothes. "How would I know?" she snarled. "You're supposed to be Master of the Beasts!"

Nearby, Elenna dragged herself out of a crater in the wet sand, soaked to the skin. Daltec hurried over and helped her to her feet. She looked at Tom. "If we don't work together," she said, "that Beast will kill us all."

Work with you? Not likely,
Tom thought. But Daltec nodded
vigorously.

"Give me the potion and one of your arrows," he told Elenna. "Electro has the blood of Krokol. In theory, Aduro's antidote should defeat him. Just as Tanner used a sword dipped in a potion, we can use an arrow!" Elenna handed a couple of her arrows to Daltec, who took a vial from his cloak, and quickly dipped the metal arrowheads in.

But Tom had heard enough. Already the metal bird was coming around for another shot at frying them alive. "'In theory'?" he sneered. "No – I'm going to stab the Beast in the heart."

Standing tall, Tom let the magical strength of his breastplate surge through his body. Then he stowed his shield on his back, and unfastened his jewelled belt.

"Now is not the time to get undressed!" shouted Ria.

Electro was soaring just above the ground, close enough to whip up eddies of sand. Tom stood his ground as the Beast flew straight towards him.

"Tom, move!" yelled Elenna.

Not yet, he thought. *Not until the last possible moment.*

Tom jumped into the air, over the Beast's head, and twisted his body at the same time. Flinging out an arm, he snagged Electro's neck with the belt, before his arms were jolted violently. He landed on the Beast's back as it soared away. Wind and rain buffeted against him from every direction. Electro's wings sparked and sizzled as they cut through the air. With a furious shriek, she carried

him upwards, away from Elenna and the others, and right into the heart of the storm.

This is it! Tom thought. *I'll kill this Beast, or I'll die! Either way, I'm ready!*

1

A DESPERATE SHOT

Shielding her eyes from the driving
rain, Elenna watched as Tom hung
on to the Beast's neck with the belt
he had looped around it. Electro
flew right into the dark clouds
overhead. Elenna could still make
out the gleaming metal bird, but
through the swirling cloud she
could barely see Tom at all.

"He's going to get himself killed!" she cried.

"Probably," Ria said. "It would be a shame, though, since this Quest is only just beginning. Whatever happens, I'm getting out of here!" The pirate girl put two fingers to her mouth and let out a piercing whistle. An instant later, her winged stallion appeared, swooping through the storm. Elenna glared at her enemy, then set off at a run towards the pyramid, placing one of Daltec's poisoned arrows in her quiver and clutching the other in her hand.

"I have to get higher," she called back to the wizard, then slung her bow over her shoulder, and started

to climb. Rainwater streamed down
the crumbling sandstone steps,
and Elenna's boots slipped again
and again on the slick rock. Before
long, blood oozed from grazes on
her palms, but she clambered on,
her eyes fixed on the sky. Lightning

illuminated the clouds above, and she caught sight of Tom hanging off the giant bird, his sword in his free hand. *Even under Ria's spell he's as brave as ever*, Elenna thought.

With a screech of anger, Electro threw back her silver wings and fell into a dive, straight towards the pyramid. Elenna took her bow from her back, but before she could aim, the huge bird rolled, exposing Tom to the pyramid's side and smashing his body against the wall. His sword spun away, clattering to the ground, and Elenna heard him give a grunt of pain. Electro swooped skywards again, then hovered for a moment, right above Elenna. Now Tom was hanging, semi-conscious, by only his belt. Lightning flashed over the Beast's wings, and she rose higher and higher, disappearing into the clouds.

If the lightning strikes Tom, he's finished...

"Do something!" Elenna shouted at Ria.

Their enemy only shrugged. "He's on his own up there, I'm afraid."

Something fell, sparkling, from the base of one of the clouds. The jewelled belt!

That means Tom must have let go...

Sure enough, his body followed, plummeting like a rock, his limbs

flailing. There was nothing to stop
him hitting the ground.

"Use Arcta's feather!" Elenna cried.
She felt a surge of relief as Tom
weakly made a grab for the shield on
his back and lifted it. Immediately, his

fall slowed and he glided away from her. But a heartbeat later, Electro let out an ear-piercing shriek and burst from the cloud too, her blazing eyes fixed on Tom.

"No, you don't!" Elenna muttered, aiming her potion-tipped arrow. She took a steadying breath. It was a desperate shot – aiming at a moving target through gale-force winds. But it was Tom's only hope.

Elenna let her arrow fly.

The arrow hit home, driving deep into the Beast's gleaming breast. Daltec's cheer carried over the howl of wind. Electro's wingbeats faltered. She let out a strangled screech. But then she turned in the

air and her luminous eyes fixed on
Elenna. As the Beast sped towards
her, Elenna could see the wicked
sharpness of Electro's beak and the
cruel curve of her huge talons. *The
arrow didn't work!*

Elenna shrank back against the steps of the pyramid, her heart pounding with fear. Lightning crackled all over the Beast's silver body. Lashes of sizzling blue energy streamed out behind her, leaving

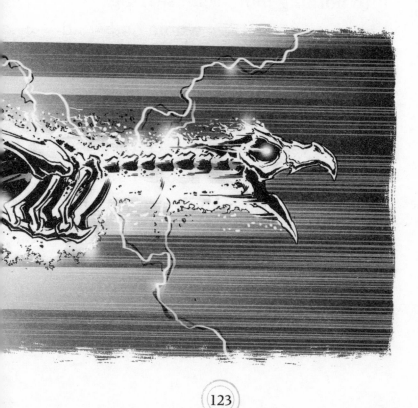

a comet-like trail in her wake. As
the Beast flew on, Elenna noticed
her metal wings losing form,
burning away at the edges. Hope
flared inside her. Elenna could see
Electro's flesh dissolving, turning
into nothing more than searing
light. Soon Electro's whole body had
transformed into a blazing streak
of blue in the sky. The light faded,
until only the bright orbs of the
Beast's eyes remained, then they too
fizzled away. *We did it. She's gone!*
Elenna thought, standing up, almost
giddy with relief. She noticed
something dropping through the air,
spinning as it fell. A silver feather. It
hit the pyramid below and tumbled

down the steep steps, coming to rest in the wet sand at the base. Elenna scrambled downwards after it.

On the ground, she could see Daltec running towards the feather too. But before he could reach it, Tom glided over the wizard's head using his shield, landing neatly and snatching the feather up.

"Tom! Give me the token!" Daltec cried, putting out his hand.

"Back off, it's mine!" Ria shrieked, diving swiftly out of the sky on the back of her flying horse. She lifted her hand and shot a fizzing ball of magical energy towards Daltec, sending him flying. As Daltec rolled on the ground, clutching his chest,

Ria landed her winged stallion at Tom's side.

"Give me the feather!" she told him.

"Don't!" Elenna screamed. But Tom shot her a disdainful sneer and

handed Ria the feather. Then he leaped up to sit behind her on the stallion's back.

"NO!" Elenna cried. *I have to stop him from going with her! I have to give him the cure!* Then she had an idea. She swiftly pulled the other arrow laced with the antidote from her quiver and aimed it at the darkly armoured figure rising above her. *If it worked on the Beast, it should work on Tom*. She targeted the gap in his shoulder armour. It was a risky shot. If the arrow struck just a few inches too high, it could hit Tom's neck and kill him. But she had to trust herself. She let fly.

Tom swivelled, and Elenna's arrow

slammed into the dark metal of his breastplate but bounced off without leaving a mark. Tom smiled.

"You always were a good shot, Elenna," Tom said. "But it will take more than arrows to stop me and my new mistress!" Then, with a swish of its broad wings, Ria's stallion leaped into the air. Elenna watched, feeling helpless, as the horse climbed quickly into the brightening sky. A single ray of sunlight pierced the clouds, hitting Tom's armour and outlining its dark silhouette, just before the winged stallion carried him out of sight.

Is this the end? Elenna thought. *Will I ever see Tom again?* But then she shook her wet hair back from her face and squared her shoulders. "One thing's for sure, while there's blood in my veins I will never give up!"

THE END

CONGRATULATIONS, YOU HAVE COMPLETED THIS QUEST!

At the end of each chapter you were awarded a special gold coin.
The QUEST in this book was worth an amazing 8 coins.

Look at the Beast Quest totem picture opposite to see how far you've come in your journey to become

MASTER OF THE BEASTS.

The more books you read, the more coins you will collect!

Do you want your own
Beast Quest Totem?

1. Cut out and collect the coin below
2. Go to the Beast Quest website
3. Download and print out your totem
4. Add your coin to the totem

www.beastquest.co.uk

READ THE BOOKS, COLLECT THE COINS!
EARN COINS FOR EVERY CHAPTER YOU READ!

550+ COINS
MASTER OF THE BEASTS

550+
515
480
445
410

410 COINS
HERO →

395
380
365
350

350 COINS
WARRIOR

320
290
260
230

230 COINS
KNIGHT →

217
206
191
180

180 COINS
SQUIRE

146
112
78
44

44 COINS
PAGE →

30
19
8

8 COINS
APPRENTICE

READ ALL THE BOOKS IN SERIES 24:
BLOOD OF THE BEAST!

BeastQuest
NEW BLOOD
ADAM BLADE

Meet three new heroes with the power to tame the Beasts!

Amy, Charlie and Sam – three children from our world – are about to discover the powerful legacy that binds them together.

They are descendants of the *Guardians of Avantia*, an elite group of heroes trained by Tom himself.

Now the time has come for a new generation to unlock the power of the Beasts and fulfil their destiny.

Read on for a sneak peek at how the Guardians first left Avantia by magic...

Karita of Banquise gazed in awe at Tom, Avantia's mighty, bearded Master of the Beasts.

Under his leadership, she and her companions would today face their greatest challenge.

Tom pointed towards the brooding Gorgonian castle. "We must recover the chest of Beast Eggs Malvel stole," he reminded them. His fierce blue eyes moved from Karita to the others. Dell of Stonewin, whose bloodline connected him to Beasts of Fire; Fern of Errinel, linked to Storm Beasts; Gustus of Colton, bonded with Water Beasts.

Malvel will be expecting an attack," Tom said. "His power is lessened, but he is still formidable." His eyes locked on Karita. "Stealth will be our greatest ally."

Karita felt as though her whole life had been a preparation for this moment. Countless hours spent studying the ancient tomes, day after day of gruelling combat training, months learning how to influence the will of Stealth Beasts and control the powers that filled the Arcane Band at her wrist.

But was she ready?

She gazed into Tom's face, and her doubts faded.

Yes!

A low rumble came from the

castle. Flashes of green lightning shot from the clouds as a swarm of screeching creatures erupted from the battlements.

Karita shuddered as Malvel's hideous minions streaked through the sky. They were man-sized, with white hides, limbs tipped with hooked claws and gaping jaws lined with sharp teeth. Their leathery wings cracked like whips.

"Karrakhs!" muttered Tom. "Karita – go!"

She nodded and slipped away behind jagged rocks. She turned to see the swarm of foul creatures engulf her companions. Tom's sword flashed. Howls rang out from the Karrakhs. The Guardians were using their Arcane Bands to form weapons that spun and slashed!

Karita raced for the castle, keeping low behind the ridge of rocks. Reaching the walls, she climbed up a gnarled vine and found a narrow window to crawl through. She looked back again. Tom and the Guardians had battled their way through the castle gates.

Well fought!

She dropped into a room and crept to the door. Torches burned in the corridor, casting shadows. The castle was silent, but Karita felt a growing dread as she slipped along the walls.

She knew where the chest of Beast eggs was hidden. But would Malvel allow her to get to them?

She came to a circular room, and
saw the chest standing by the wall.
Her heart hammering, Karita opened
the lid and gazed down at the eggs.
They were different sizes, shapes and
colours. One slipped from the pile
and she caught it in her gloved hand.
It was pale blue, about the size of
a goose egg. Acting on instinct, she
slipped it inside her breastplate.

Crash!

She spun around. Malvel stood
against the room's closed door.

"Did you really think you could
enter my domain unseen?" he
snarled, a green glow igniting in his
palm. His voice was weaker than
she'd imagined. "I *wanted* you to
come here. After all, only a Guardian

can hatch a Beast Egg."

Karita swallowed hard, seeking a way to escape.

"You and your friends will hatch these Beasts and I will drink in their power," growled the wizard. "I will become mighty again and Avantia will bow before me!"

"I'm not afraid of you!" Karita shouted.

A ball of green fire exploded from Malvel's hand. Karita dived aside, seared by the heat.

She leaped up, thrusting her right arm towards the wizard. The Arcane Band began to form a weapon, but another blast of fire sent her sliding across the floor.

Malvel loomed over her, both hands

burning green. Before he could strike, the door burst open and Tom and the Guardians rushed into the room.

"No!" roared Malvel. "Where are my Karrakhs?"

"Defeated!" shouted Tom, whirling his sword to deflect Malvel's green flames. "Guardians! Take the eggs!"

Fern dived for the chest, but a blast from the wizard knocked her over.

"The eggs are mine!" howled Malvel. He traced a large circle of fire in the air. There was a blast of hot wind as the flaming hoop crackled and spat.

Malvel snatched up the chest and turned to the heart of the fiery circle.

"He's opened a portal!" shouted

Tom. "Stop him!"

Gustus ran at the wizard and wrested the chest from his grip. Roaring in anger, Malvel launched a fireball, but Fern managed to shove Gustus out of its path. But the force of her push knocked Gustus into the portal. With a stifled cry, he and the chest of eggs were gone.

"No!" Fern shouted, diving in after him. With a yell, Dell ran after her.

"Wait!" shouted Tom.

"It's our duty to protect the eggs!" Dell called back as he disappeared into the swirling portal.

Malvel sprang forward, but Tom bounded in front of him, holding him back with his spinning blade as the wizard hurled magical fireballs.

Karita saw the walls of the portal writhing and distorting. Malvel's fireballs were making it unstable. At any moment it might vanish!

Tom was knocked back by a torrent of green fire as the wizard turned and leaped into the portal. Karita flung herself after him.

"No! Karita!" The last thing she heard was Tom's voice. "The portal is in flux! You could be sent anywhere!"

And then there was nothing but a rushing wind and howling darkness, as she plunged into the unknown.

Look out for
Beast Quest: New Blood
to find out what happens next!

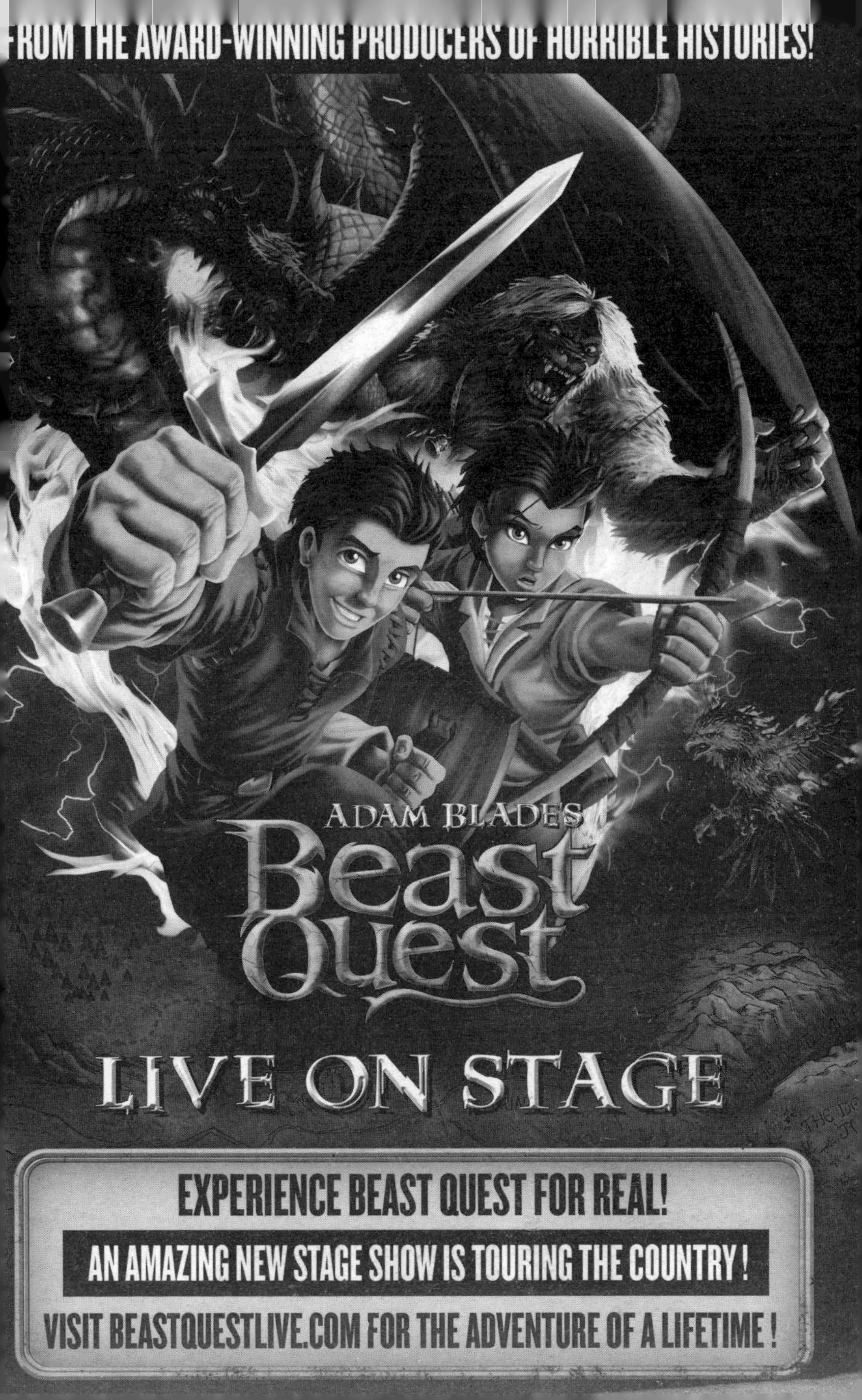
FROM THE AWARD-WINNING PRODUCERS OF HORRIBLE HISTORIES!
ADAM BLADE'S
Beast Quest
LIVE ON STAGE
EXPERIENCE BEAST QUEST FOR REAL!
AN AMAZING NEW STAGE SHOW IS TOURING THE COUNTRY !
VISIT BEASTQUESTLIVE.COM FOR THE ADVENTURE OF A LIFETIME !